NEVER TAKE A SHARK TO THE DENTIST

(and other things not to do)

NEVER TAKE A SHARK TO THE DENTIST

(and other things not to do)

by JUDI BARRETT with art by JOHN NICKLE

SCHOLASTIC INC.

New York Toronto London Auckland Sydney Mexico City New Delhi Hong Kong

To Sasha —J. B.

To Brianna —J. N.

Never take a shark to the dentist.

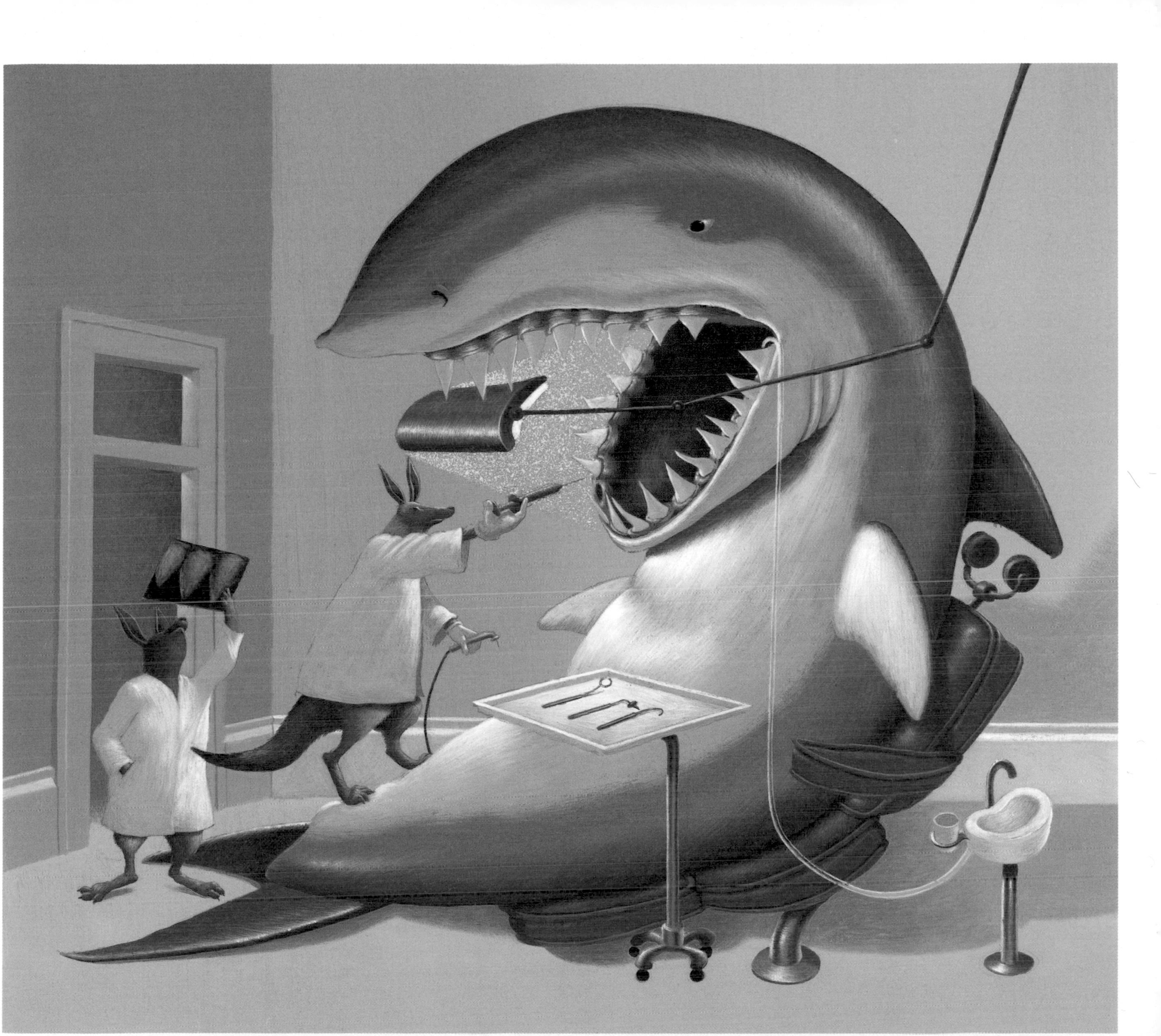

Never **sit next to a porcupine on the subway.**

AMPHIBIAN
ACNE
1-800 FROGZIT
TRIBUNE

Never **go shopping for shoes with a centipede.**

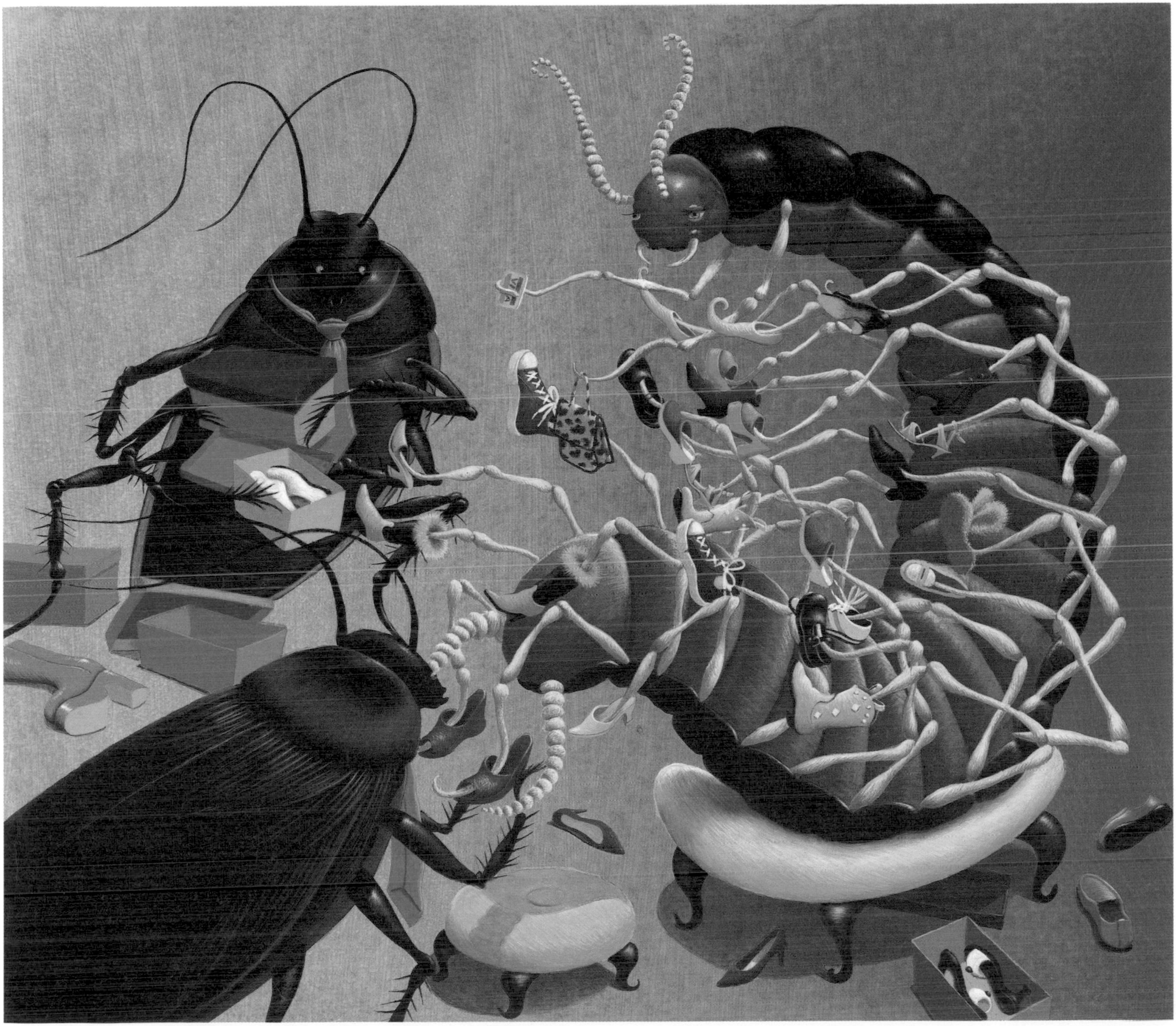

Never **knit a hat for a moose.**

Never invite an ant to a picnic.

Never **take a giraffe to the movies.**

Never **play checkers with a spider.**

Never share your lunch with a pig.

JUICE

Never **play double Dutch with a grasshopper.**

Never **hold hands with a lobster.**

Never take a goat with you to the library.

Ga to Go

Never **give a moth a sweater for her birthday.**

Never **go to the bank with a raccoon.**

But *always* go shopping with a pelican.

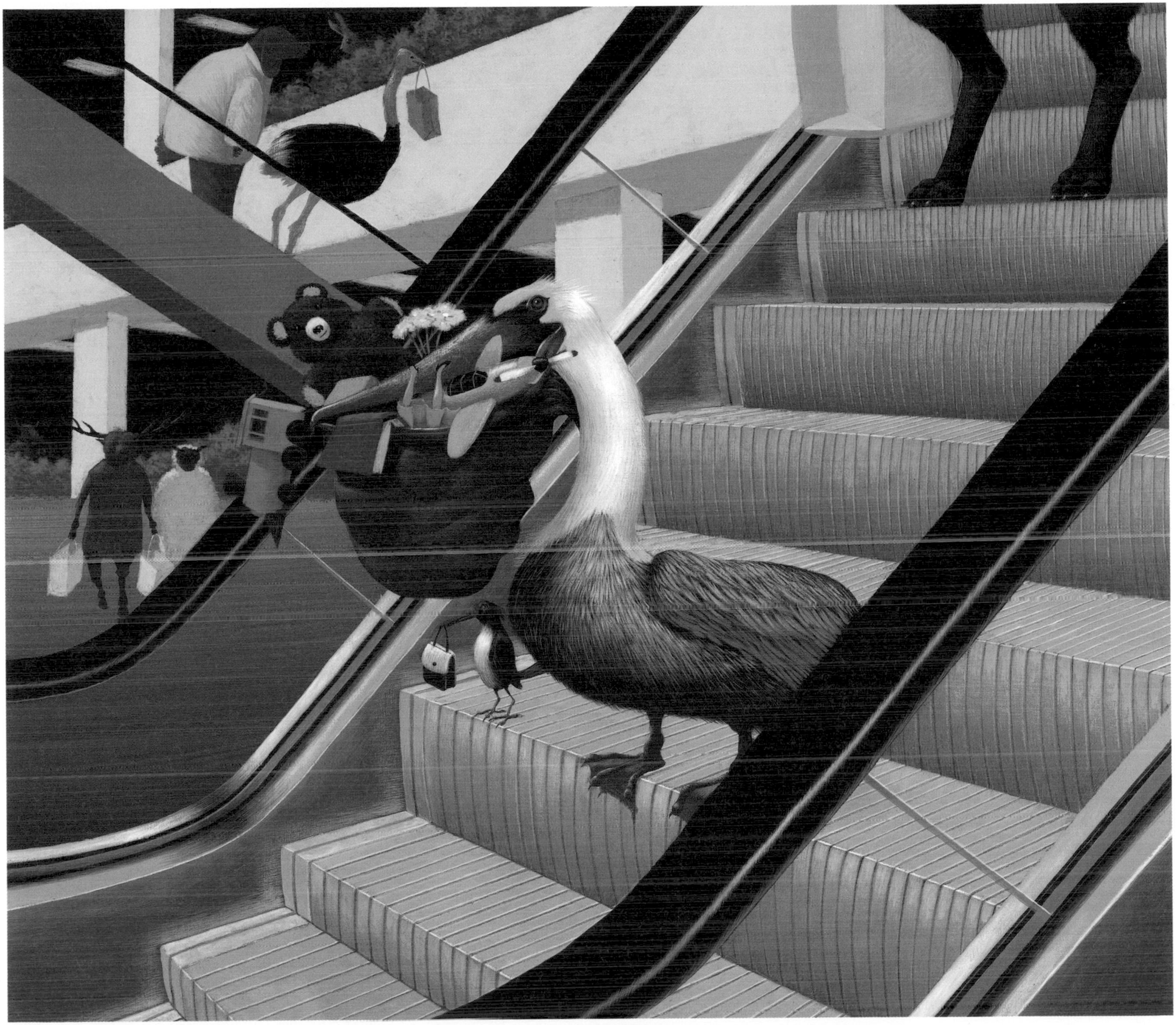

ISBN 978-0-545-24834-1

12 11 10 9 8 7 6 5 4 3 2 1 10 11 12 13 14 15/0

Printed in the U.S.A. 40

This edition first printing, January 2010

Book design by Michael McCartney

The text for this book is set in Matrix and Matrix Script.

The illustrations for this book were rendered in acrylic paint.